BIBLEMAN
THE ANIMATED ADVENTURES

SPOILING THE SCHEMES OF LUXOR SPAWNDROTH
An Adventure in Self-Control

FREE TO PLAY!

Storylines by Wayne Zeitner
Adaptations by Caroline Slemp

Copyright © 2017 by B&H Publishing Group. All rights reserved.
Character ownership and licensing by P23 Entertainment Inc.
ISBN: 978-1-4627-6151-7
Published by B&H Publishing Group, Nashville, Tennessee
DEWEY: C153.8   SUBHD: BIBLE. N.T. STORIES \
TEMPTATION \ SELF-CONTROL
Unless otherwise noted, all Scripture references are taken
from the Christian Standard Bible (CSB).
Copyright © 2017 by Holman Bible Publishers,
Nashville, Tennessee. All rights reserved.
Printed in Shenzhen, Guangdong,
China in June 2017.
1 2 3 4 5   21 20 19 18 17

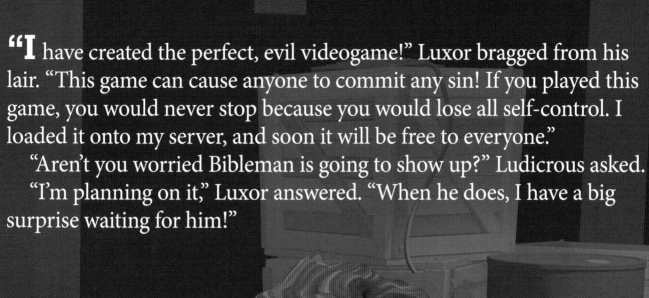

"I have created the perfect, evil videogame!" Luxor bragged from his lair. "This game can cause anyone to commit any sin! If you played this game, you would never stop because you would lose all self-control. I loaded it onto my server, and soon it will be free to everyone."

"Aren't you worried Bibleman is going to show up?" Ludicrous asked.

"I'm planning on it," Luxor answered. "When he does, I have a big surprise waiting for him!"

That afternoon, Luxor's video game was a hit at the mall.

Ludicrous called out to shoppers, "Sleepovers, play dates, hanging out, hanging in—any time is a good time for *Spawndroth*! And the best part is that it's free!"

Tom checked out the game. "What device is it for?" he asked Luxor.

"*Spawndroth* can be played on any device that connects to the internet," Luxor answered.

"So, what's the catch?" some girls asked.

"There's no catch," Luxor said grinning. "*Spawndroth* is simply all yours for free."

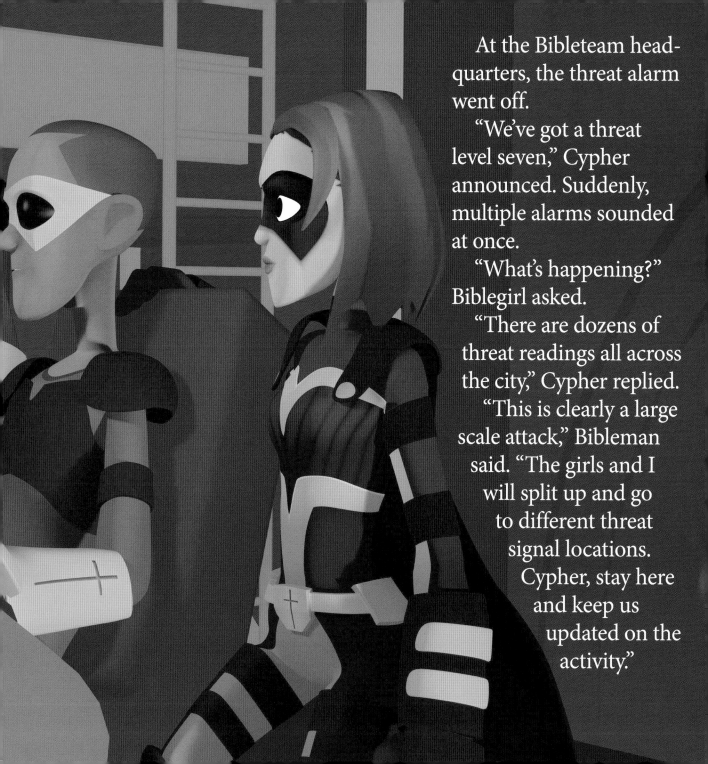

At the Bibleteam head-quarters, the threat alarm went off.

"We've got a threat level seven," Cypher announced. Suddenly, multiple alarms sounded at once.

"What's happening?" Biblegirl asked.

"There are dozens of threat readings all across the city," Cypher replied.

"This is clearly a large scale attack," Bibleman said. "The girls and I will split up and go to different threat signal locations. Cypher, stay here and keep us updated on the activity."

Bibleman went to the first threat signal location. Tom's mother led Bibleman to where her family played a video game.

"I'm so glad you're here, Bibleman," she said. "They've been playing *Spawndroth* like they're zombies!"

"*Spawndroth*! Why am I not surprised?" Bibleman said. "Excuse me, boys; you need to stop playing that game. We believe it's dangerous." Neither the boys nor their father paid him any attention.

Melody radioed in. "I'm with two girls who can't stop playing a video game," she said.

"Luxor Spawndroth is responsible," Bibleman explained. "The game makes players lose their self-control."

Cypher buzzed in. "The only way to stop it is to shut down the server, which GPS shows is in Luxor's hideout."

"Let's all meet up there," Bibleman said.

At Luxor's lair, the Bibleteam found a large computer.

"This must be the server," Cypher said. "We need to plug this memory stick into it and replace the game with a Bible lesson."

"Everyone, keep alert," Bibleman warned. "There's a reason Luxor has brought us back to his hideout."

"Do you think it's a trap?" Melody asked.

"Definitely," Bibleman said. "Cypher, did the Bible lesson upload?"

"No, I'm completely locked out of the system," Cypher replied.

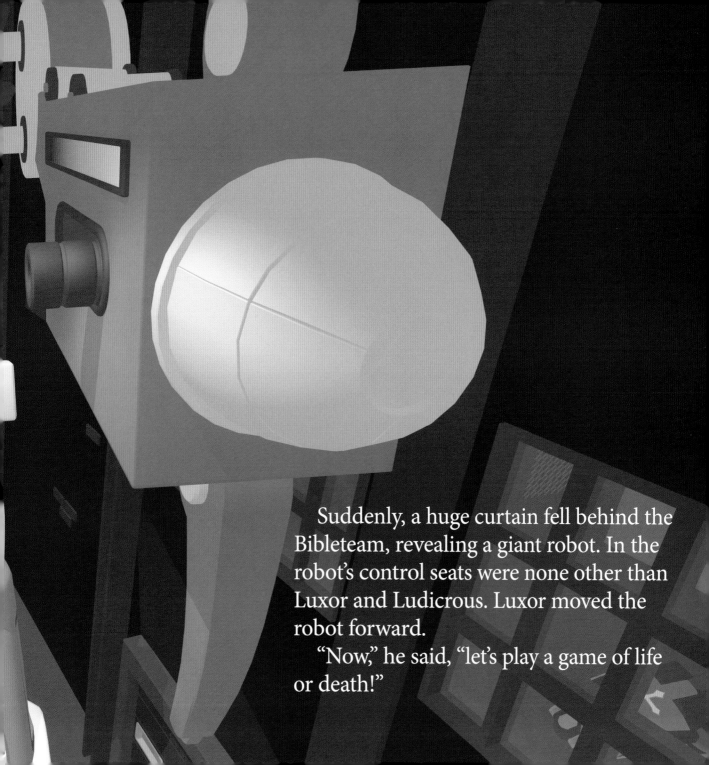

Suddenly, a huge curtain fell behind the Bibleteam, revealing a giant robot. In the robot's control seats were none other than Luxor and Ludicrous. Luxor moved the robot forward.

"Now," he said, "let's play a game of life or death!"

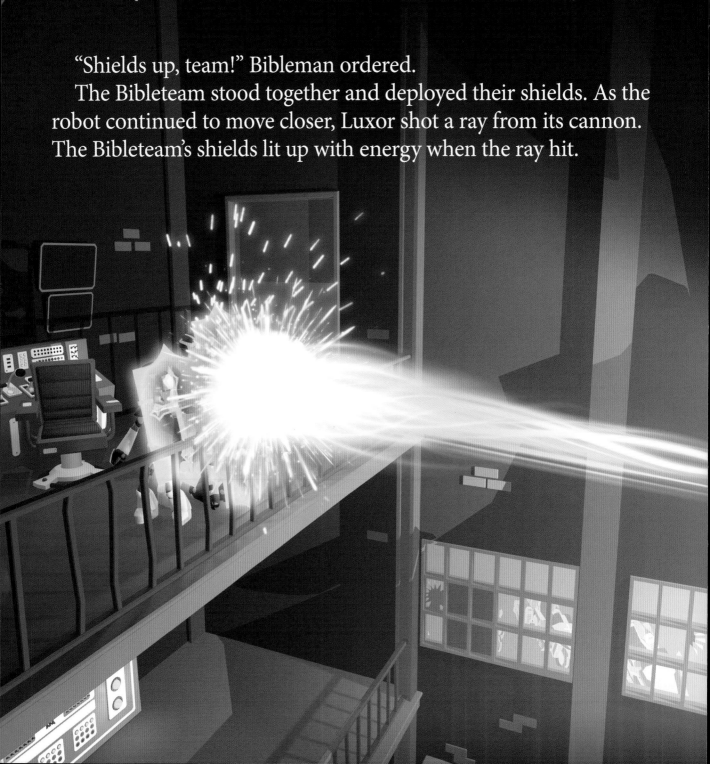

"Shields up, team!" Bibleman ordered.

The Bibleteam stood together and deployed their shields. As the robot continued to move closer, Luxor shot a ray from its cannon. The Bibleteam's shields lit up with energy when the ray hit.

"Everyone, repeat Philippians 4:13!" Bibleman shouted.

"I am able to do all things through him who strengthens me!" the team said together.

The ray bounced off their shields and shot back toward the robot.

"You think Scripture will save you?" Luxor scoffed. "Let's see how you handle this!"

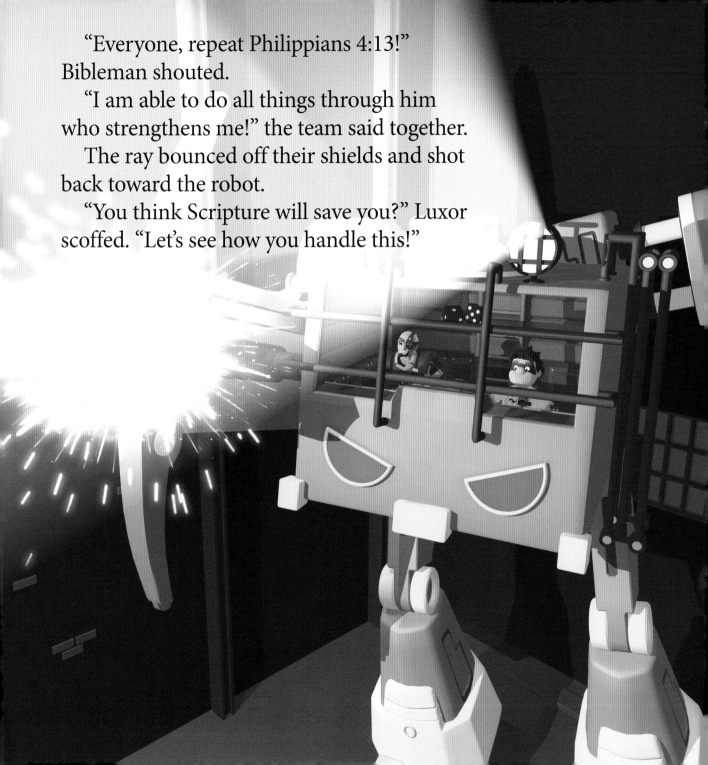

Luxor fired the robot's cannon again. An even bigger ray of swirling energy blasted at the Bibleteam. The Bibleteam jumped out of the way. The energy ball hit the computer. It surged and then went black.

"Get to the Biblevan, now!" Bibleman said.

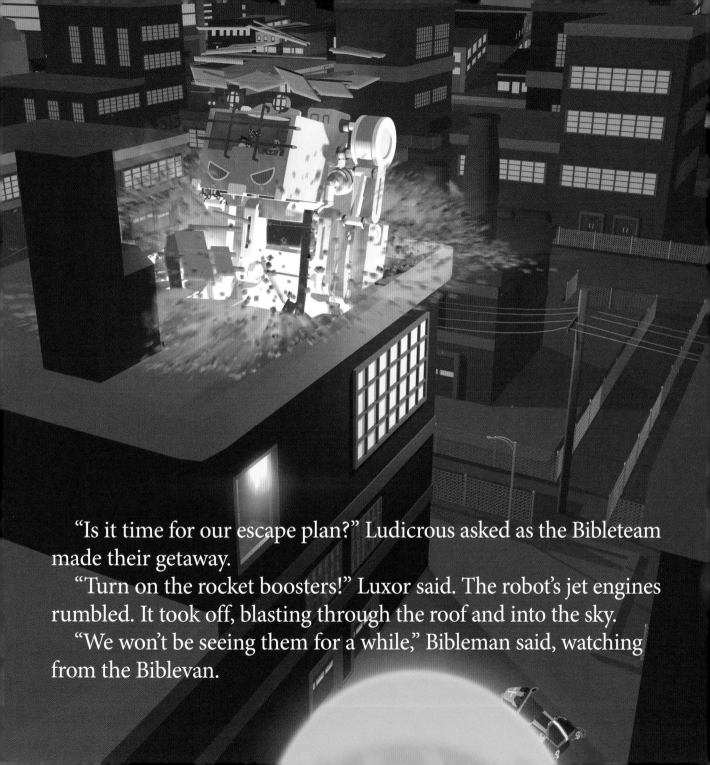

"Is it time for our escape plan?" Ludicrous asked as the Bibleteam made their getaway.

"Turn on the rocket boosters!" Luxor said. The robot's jet engines rumbled. It took off, blasting through the roof and into the sky.

"We won't be seeing them for a while," Bibleman said, watching from the Biblevan.

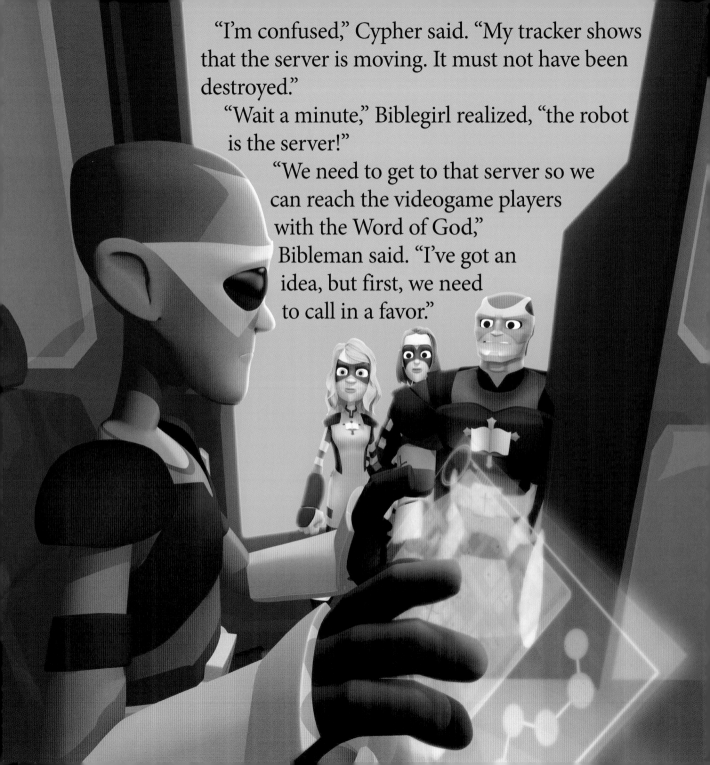

"I'm confused," Cypher said. "My tracker shows that the server is moving. It must not have been destroyed."

"Wait a minute," Biblegirl realized, "the robot is the server!"

"We need to get to that server so we can reach the videogame players with the Word of God," Bibleman said. "I've got an idea, but first, we need to call in a favor."

After landing the robot, Ludicrous turned on the TV. "Boss, Dan Noteman is talking about *Spawndroth*!" Ludicrous exclaimed.

"If anyone knows the genius behind this success, I want to talk to them," the talk show host said.

"Call that studio!" Luxor ordered. "This is the moment I go viral!"

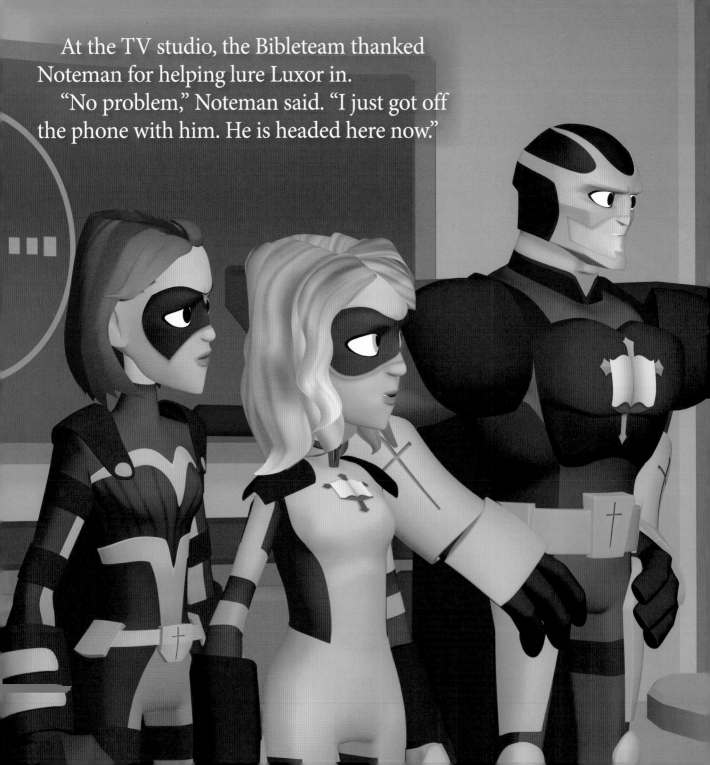

At the TV studio, the Bibleteam thanked Noteman for helping lure Luxor in.

"No problem," Noteman said. "I just got off the phone with him. He is headed here now."

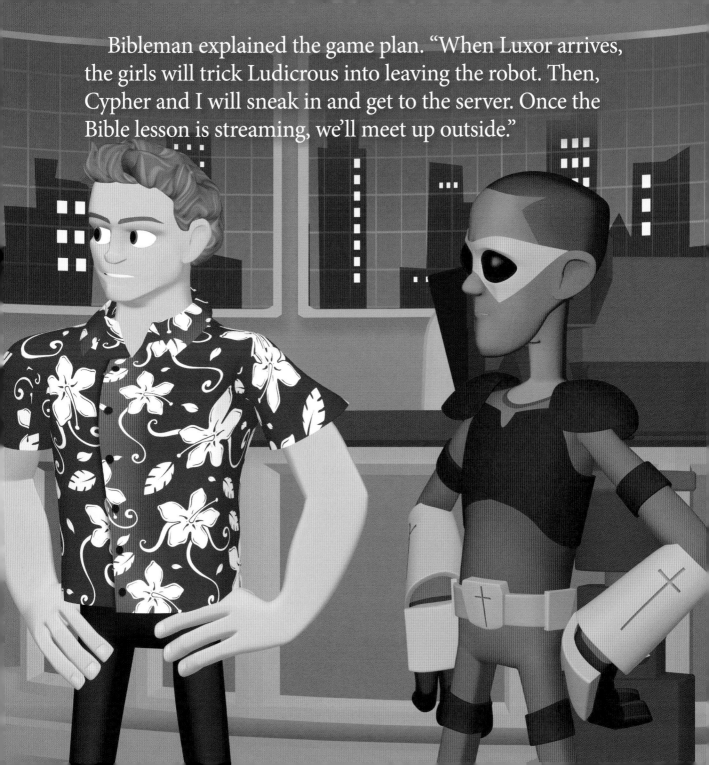

Bibleman explained the game plan. "When Luxor arrives, the girls will trick Ludicrous into leaving the robot. Then, Cypher and I will sneak in and get to the server. Once the Bible lesson is streaming, we'll meet up outside."

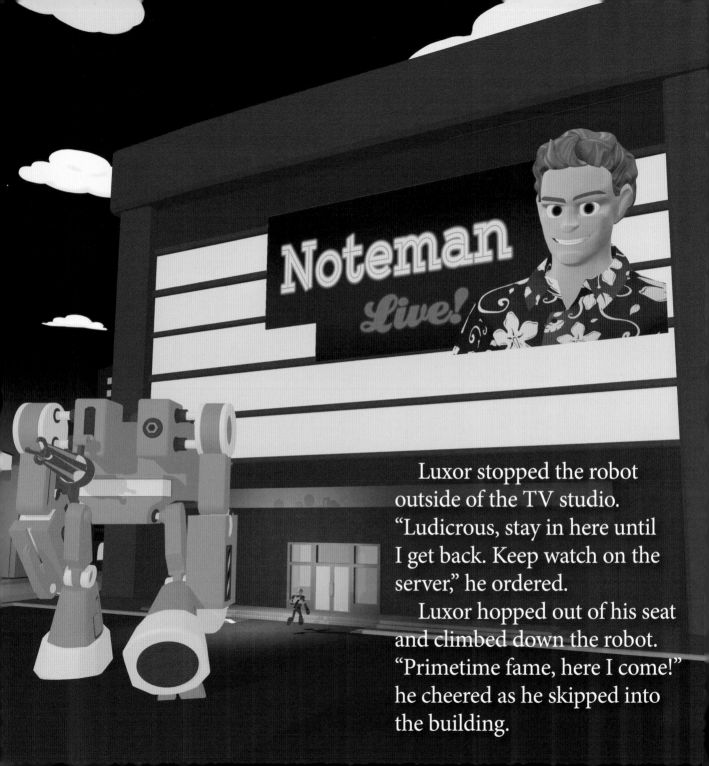

Luxor stopped the robot outside of the TV studio. "Ludicrous, stay in here until I get back. Keep watch on the server," he ordered.

Luxor hopped out of his seat and climbed down the robot. "Primetime fame, here I come!" he cheered as he skipped into the building.

Inside the robot, Ludicrous's stomach growled. "Oh, I'm so hungry. I haven't gotten to eat all day," he complained.

Just then, Biblegirl and Melody, dressed in disguises, called to him from outside the studio. "If you're with the show, there's free pizza inside!"

Ludicrous's stomach growled again. "I'll be back before Luxor even knows I'm gone!" he said.

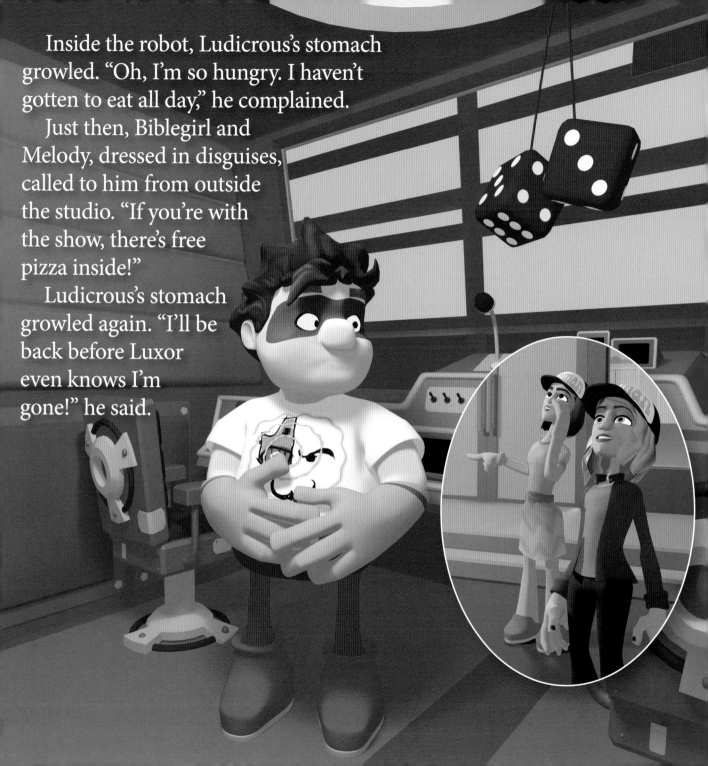

As soon as Ludicrous went into the studio, Bibleman and Cypher snuck into the robot. Cypher quickly found the server and plugged the memory stick into it. "Goodbye, *Spawndroth*. Hello, Bible lesson! It's show time!" he said.

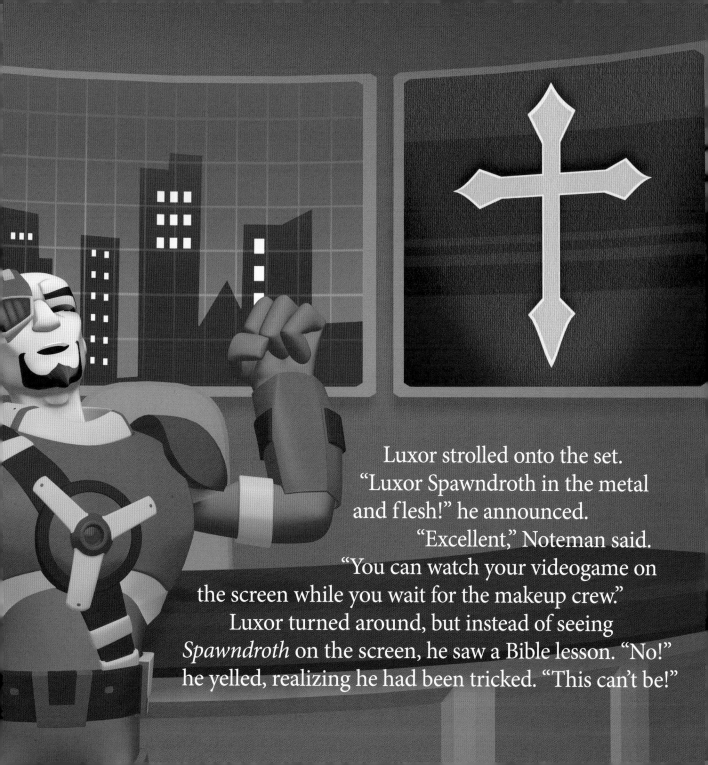

Luxor strolled onto the set. "Luxor Spawndroth in the metal and flesh!" he announced.

"Excellent," Noteman said. "You can watch your videogame on the screen while you wait for the makeup crew."

Luxor turned around, but instead of seeing *Spawndroth* on the screen, he saw a Bible lesson. "No!" he yelled, realizing he had been tricked. "This can't be!"

The Bible lesson played all across the city.
"Jesus had been praying for forty days and hadn't stopped to eat once. Satan tempted Him to turn stones into bread. Jesus said, 'Man must not live on bread alone, but on the Word of God.'"

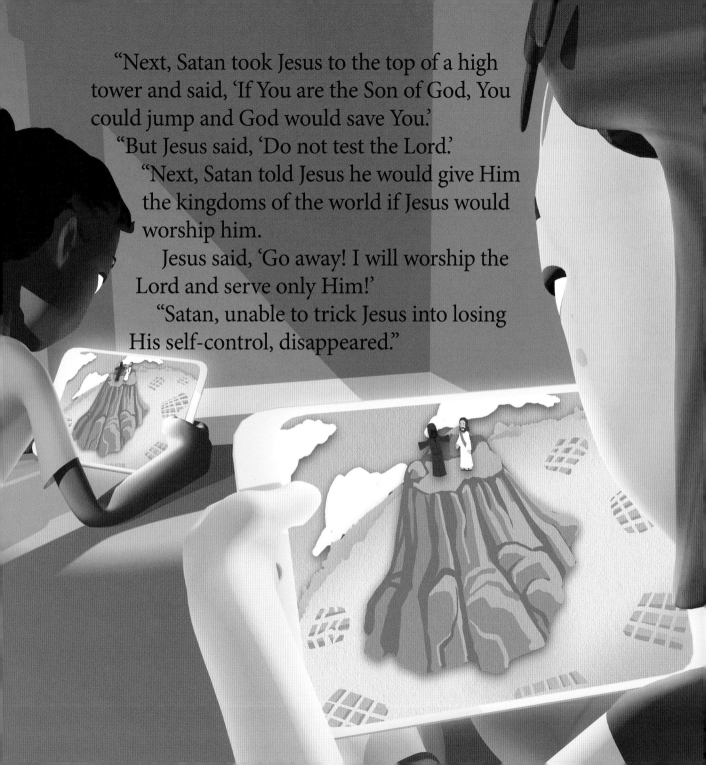

"Next, Satan took Jesus to the top of a high tower and said, 'If You are the Son of God, You could jump and God would save You.'

"But Jesus said, 'Do not test the Lord.'

"Next, Satan told Jesus he would give Him the kingdoms of the world if Jesus would worship him.

Jesus said, 'Go away! I will worship the Lord and serve only Him!'

"Satan, unable to trick Jesus into losing His self-control, disappeared."

After watching the Bible lesson, the boys and their father realized they had lost their self-control.

"Mom, I'm sorry. I could hear you telling us to stop, but I just couldn't," Tom said.

"It's okay. Thanks to Bibleman, everything is going to be alright now," she assured him.

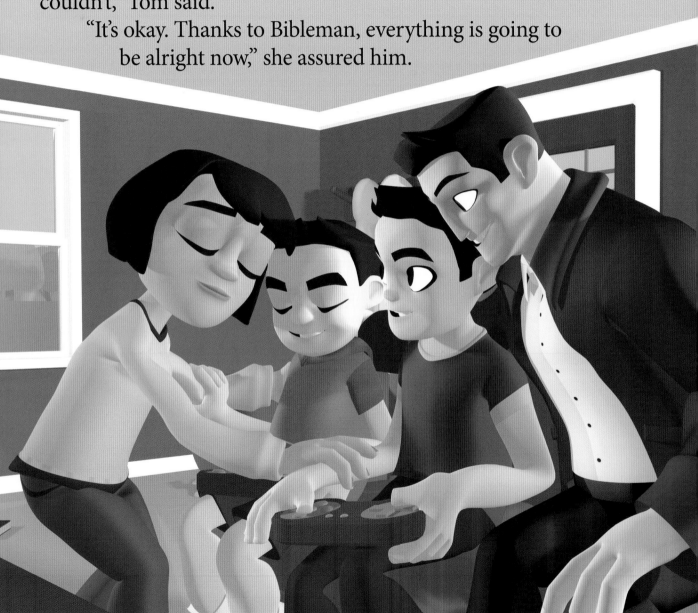

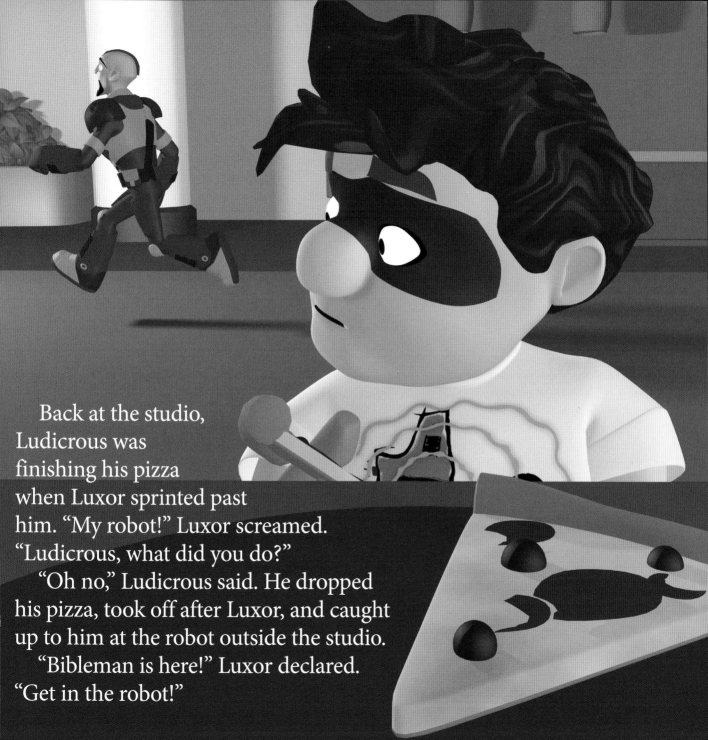

Back at the studio, Ludicrous was finishing his pizza when Luxor sprinted past him. "My robot!" Luxor screamed. "Ludicrous, what did you do?"

"Oh no," Ludicrous said. He dropped his pizza, took off after Luxor, and caught up to him at the robot outside the studio.

"Bibleman is here!" Luxor declared. "Get in the robot!"

The Bibleteam approached, wielding their weapons, just as the villains made it inside the robot.

"Your game is over, Luxor," Bibleman announced.

Luxor sneered, "Once I crush you with my robot, *Spawndroth* will be back!"

"You still don't get it," Bibleman said. "The Word of God is all anyone needs to defeat you."

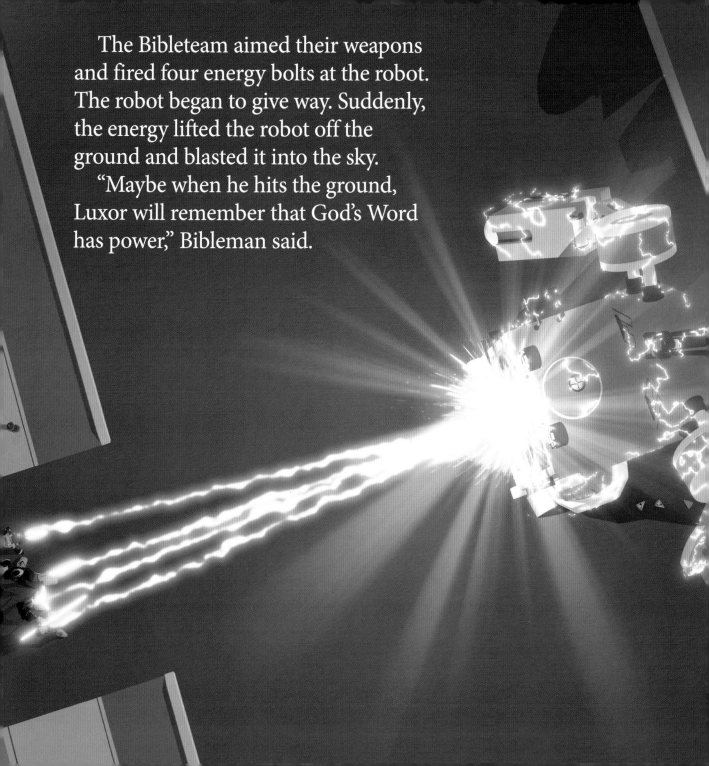

The Bibleteam aimed their weapons and fired four energy bolts at the robot. The robot began to give way. Suddenly, the energy lifted the robot off the ground and blasted it into the sky.

"Maybe when he hits the ground, Luxor will remember that God's Word has power," Bibleman said.

Remember

"Therefore, submit to God. Resist the Devil, and he will flee from you."
—James 4:7

Read

Read Matthew 4:1–11. In this passage, Satan tempts Jesus to believe
that Satan's ideas are better than God's. However, Jesus isn't fooled
because He knows that God's commands are best. When you are
tempted, just remember that God loves us and His commands are
good. God gives us the strength to face any challenge.

Think

1. When you feel tempted, what can you remember about God?
2. Describe a time you felt God's strength when you were tempted to
   disobey.
3. How many verses can you find about self-control? (Hint: start with
   Galatians 5:22–23 and 1 Corinthians 9:25)

God's Word has power over temptation!